The night Maryam met Santa Claus

Part 1
True News

Maha Gabir

Dedication

I dedicate this book to my dear father's soul. I love you Dad, I hope you are proud of me, just as I was always proud of you.

R.I.P.

Table Of Contents

Chapter 1

The Night Maryam Met Santa Claus

"True news! Good news!" I shouted happily as I was getting out of my father's car, holding an iPad in my left hand and waving to my friends with my right.

My friends were gathered at the school door, waving back at me and eagerly awaiting my true and good news.

They stood in front of the school door beside my uncle Ahmed, the old doorman, who was leaning on his big, dark brown cane and opening the school door. It was the first day after the Christmas and New Year holidays.

"How was your holiday, Maryam?" asked my friend Aisha. "Did you visit your cousins in America?"

Hugging them all with open arms, I said, "Yes, guys, it was an incredible holiday." I continued, "But guess what the news is!"

They chanted in unison, with hysterical screams, "Santa! Santa! Santa! Santa!" Then we joyfully jumped and held each other.

After we finished our celebration, my friend Eman said, "Please, Maryam, tell us how you met Santa Claus! Please tell us before the bell rings; we can't wait."

We then moved to the schoolyard and sat in our favorite place: the biggest, loveliest tree in the school, a Baobab tree called "Tabaldi Tree." The reason we liked it so much is that we felt we had a deep and loving relationship with it, and it was affectionate to us. It fed us every day, and we often picked its fruits and ate them for lunch. It was like a family relationship to us; the tree kept our secrets and took part in our adventures, It felt happy when we were happy and sad when we were sad. It was our shelter,

too; it protected us from the heat of the sun and from the rain. It shared our school life with us.

When we all sat down, I took a deep breath and stared at the tree leaves for a second. Then I said: "The faith!" and continued. "If you have deep faith in God's help, your dream will come true."

After I had uttered those last words, the bell rang, and all the students left quickly to their classrooms.

Meeting with my friends and sharing this excitement, I forgot to introduce myself! My name is Maryam; I am a 9-year old girl, and I live in Africa with my parents. We decided to visit my cousins in America for the Christmas and New Year holidays. My aunt has lived in America a long time with her family (her husband and three kids), but they've never come back to Africa since they left.

The ultimate thing that grabbed my attention in America was that I actually got to meet Santa Claus on Christmas Eve.

After I saw a movie about Santa Claus, I asked my cousins about him, and I was soon crazy about him. My cousins told me many stories about Santa Claus and the gifts he used to bring to them, and how eagerly they waited on the morning of every 25th of December to open their presents.

I wondered why Santa Claus did not visit my friends and I. I had never heard about him—not

in my country, or in my town—so I was eager to go to America, not because I wanted gifts from Santa Claus, but because I wanted to show him it was not fair that he didn't visit my country. I wanted to show him that there should be some equality in Christmas, even if we do not get a toy.

I had told my friends about my plan, and my intention to meet Santa Claus when visiting my cousins. They all asked me to ask Santa Claus politely to visit, and to bring them gifts too.

The day before I set off on my trip, my friends gathered at my house to say goodbye and to send their innocent wishes with me to give to Santa Claus.

Aisha had always told us about her dream to be a professional volleyball player, so she asked Santa for a volleyball. Aya, who was always documenting our diaries with drawings, needed a paint set. Eman wanted children's books because she loved reading so much and we did not have a library at school or in our neighborhood. And Minna, the most talented student in the school at music, wanted a violin.

I kept all their wishes in my mind and heart and said goodbye to them.

Chapter 2

The next day, we headed for America.

While we were on the plane, significant questions were playing in my mind: What will I say to Santa Claus when I see him? What are the right questions to ask him? Will he be kind to me or not? Will he be happy with all my questions, and will he answer them all? Despite being a little bit worried about whether or not I would succeed, I was still so excited.

By nature, I like meeting new people. I love to open up and chat with people from anywhere in the world. I believe God created us to know and meet each other, to share our ideas, and not to distance ourselves from one another.

On the plane, I chatted with the flight attendant about many things, like my school, friends, and family.

She asked me, "So, are you visiting America to see your cousins, honey?"

I looked at her with open eyes, and for a while, with a silent sight, I thought about my secret reason. I hesitated to tell her about what was on my mind, because I did not know if she would understand me or ignore my idea—and if she did, it would disappoint me.

I took a deep breath and said, "I would like to tell you something, but you have to promise me you will never tell anyone about it, and keep it just between us."

She answered me with careful attention and a smiling face. "Sure, sweetheart. It will be between you and me."

Then I looked right and left, wanting to be sure that my parents were sleeping, because if they knew, they would say I was crazy. Then I told her, "I am going to meet Santa Claus."

"Santa Claus...?" The flight attendant was surprised.

At first, I felt uncomfortable with her reaction. I started to blame myself: Why did I tell my secret to a stranger? Nobody will understand me! But the flight attendant recognized the reaction on my face, and immediately, she said, "Oh, my sweetheart, I also dream of meeting Santa Claus one day!"

Her reaction gave me peace of mind. I adjusted my seat and said happily, "Really?"

The flight attendant said, "Yes, honey, my kids and I wait every year for Santa Claus to visit our house."

I asked with interest, "Does Santa Claus visit you every year?"

"Yes."

"Have you ever met him?"

"Never."

"Why?"

"Because if Santa Claus finds you awake, he will never come to your house again."

"Does he bring gifts?"

"Sometimes, yes; sometimes, no. Sometimes he will just leave us with cards."

"How come?" I asked.

She replied, "If my kids do not behave well, Santa Claus does not bring gifts."

"How does he know?"

"God has given Santa Claus the gift of knowing everything!"

"How many kids do you have?"

"Two—one girl and one boy." The flight attendant brought out her wallet and showed me a photo of her kids.

I said, "They are so cute!"

She said, "You are also very pretty and cute."

I answered shyly, "Thanks."

The flight attendant left me to sleep because the distance was so far. Later, I was awoken by my mother's voice. "Honey! Honey, are you having a dream? Why are you talking while you are sleeping?"

I answered, with a sleepy voice, "what did I say?"

"You said, 'Santa, Santa, Santa...'," my mother replied.

I smiled and started snoozing again. After a while, my mother woke me once more and told me not to sleep because we were about to land.

I woke up and went to the restroom with my mother. When we came back, we sat in our seats. I was so excited! Finally, I would reach the country where my dreams would come true.

After landing, all the passengers left, but I ran to the crews' cabinet and hugged the flight attendant. I whispered to her, "I will tell Santa Claus you want to meet him."

The flight attendant said, with a smiling face, "I will miss you, honey. I have enjoyed meeting you very much." Then she got her mobile and took a selfie with me and said, "Goodbye, and I hope your dream comes true."

Chapter 3

When I arrived in America, there were only five days until Christmas; my small dream just controlled my mind. I had never met my cousins before; this was the first time. My cousins were two boys and a girl: 4-year-old Ibrahim and 9-year-old Yousuf, and 6-year-old Hawa. I was so happy to meet them. Because I am an only

child, I considered them to be my own sister and brothers.

I did not tell them about my small dream and what I was planning to do on Christmas Eve. I thought if I told them, they would not allow me to do it; I still remembered what the flight attendant told me, so I realized I couldn't tell anyone about my plan.

My aunt's family house was a beautiful two-story home. The first level contained a big living room with a kitchen, master bedroom, and guest room. The second level had three bedrooms, and there was a big beautiful backyard, with a bascule and a basketball hoop for the kids.

One day, when we were playing in the backyard, the weather was so lovely, and I liked their backyard so much because in the corner, there was a big tree that reminded me of my friends and my school too.

I was sitting with Hawa under the tree, watching Yousuf and Ibrahim playing soccer.

I asked Hawa, "What is the name of this tree?"

She looked at me and said, "Ew! Why do you speak English with a strange accent, Maryam?" She continued with a laugh, "I have wanted to ask you this since the first day I met you."

When her brothers heard her question, they stopped playing and came to us.

I answered, "Because it is not my mother tongue." They all laughed.

I asked, "What is so funny, guys? It is good that I speak English. I can speak English at this age only because I went to an American nursery and pre-school."

"And now your elementary school is also an American school?" said Ibrahim.

"No, I go to a public school in the neighborhood, because the American school is so expensive."

"So, not all people speak English in your country?" asked Hawa.

"It depends on their education; my parents wanted me to speak English, so they sent me there when I was little," I said.

They all continued laughing, but I kept silent. I realized on that day how difficult it was to communicate with my cousins. They were so different from me and thought differently of me, and even of my friends at school.

They were trying to make fun of me with every conversation, and continued laughing at everything I said. I didn't like that, so I cut the conversation short, and I didn't have any more such long talks with them.

Chapter 4

I knew that my cousins had sent letters to Santa Claus, but I didn't want to ask them about it. I heard them talking about it when we were watching a movie on TV. I was thinking about how to send a letter to Santa Claus. I needed to send him a letter, but how? And I was almost running out of time.

"Maryam, honey, come with me to the store," my aunt said, interrupting my thoughts, and continued, "I want to buy some things."

I nodded and left with her.

In the store, I saw a table with small cards and a pen on it, and beside it, there was a big red box with a small crack on the top.

"What is that, Aunt?" I asked.

"Kids send letters to Santa Claus and put them in that box," Aunt answered.

At that moment, I felt my small heart stop beating: what I was thinking of and hoping for was right before my eyes! All I said inside myself at that time was, "I love you, God, you are always with me." Without hesitation, I took the pen and a card from the table and started writing my letter to Santa Claus.

DEAR SANTA CLAUS,

MY NAME IS MARYAM. I CAME FROM AFRICA TO MEET YOU. I HEARD FROM MY COUSINS THAT YOU COME EVERY CHRISTMAS EVE. I HAVE ALSO HEARD THAT YOU DON'T LIKE TO FIND PEOPLE AWAKE WHEN YOU VISIT. BUT PLEASE CAN YOU ACCEPT ME AS A SPECIAL CASE AS I HAVE COME ALL THE WAY FROM AFRICA ESPECIALLY TO SEE YOU? THIS IS THE BIGGEST DREAM OF MY LIFE, AND I HAVE WISHES FROM MY FRIENDS TO YOU. SO PLEASE PLEASE PLEASE MAKE ALL OUR DREAMS COME TRUE.

THANK YOU,

MARYAM.

Then I put the letter in the box, saying "Please, God, as you let me send a letter to Santa easily, let me meet him easily."

Chapter 5

So far, my holiday was going well, except the constant bullying from my cousins. But I didn't care about that, because my mind was wholly occupied with one idea: Santa's World. I was trying to avoid any aggression, and I somehow succeeded in ignoring my cousins' bullying.

The next day, when we were having lunch, I asked Yousuf, "What was the last gift Santa Claus brought to you?"

He answered, "Bicycle," and he said with a laugh, "Do you want Santa Claus to bring a gift for you?"

I answered wonderingly ,"Why not? I sent him a letter."

He said, surprisingly, "How and when?"

I wondered at his reaction, but I said, "Yesterday, when I went to the store with Aunty."

He said, "Santa Claus does not bring gifts for people from Africa." They all laughed loudly, and he continued, "If he wants to give gifts to Africans, why doesn't he go there?"

I kept silent. I didn't know what to say; he was totally right, because this is why I wanted to come here. I wanted to ask Santa Claus one question. I don't want gifts like my friends, I want to know why he doesn't visit us in Africa. Yousuf's comments broke my heart; I felt so bad.

At this time, my mother called for all, "Dinner is ready." After dinner, all the family sat in the living room, talking and chatting.

"So, how are you, dear Maryam?" asked my Aunt's husband.

I said, "I am good, thank God."

"She must be good because she is in America," said Hawa; then all my cousins, as usual, laughed.

I said to them, "Even when I was in Africa, I was also good, among my family, our neighbors, and friends."

I couldn't tell my aunt's husband why I was feeling so bad, and how I found my cousins behaving differently than I do. Due to the way that my cousins treated me, from that time, I thought all American people didn't like African people. Maybe that is why Santa Claus doesn't come to Africa!

Chapter 6

The next day, I woke up early and prepared myself to go to the market with my Aunt to do some shopping for Christmas dinner. It was two days until Christmas Eve.

"Honey, are you ready?" asked my Aunt while she was knocking on the door.

"Yes, Aunt," I said.

I sat silently in the back seat in my Aunt's car. All the way, my Aunt was trying to talk to me and know why I was upset, but I said one word: "Nothing."

When we arrived at the market, I got out of the car, and my aunt held my hand as we headed to the market.

At the door, there was a lady coming from the other side pushing a shopping cart. She wanted to go out quickly, and she opened the door, but my leg hit the shopping cart and I fell down. I screamed in pain when my head hit the floor. The lady pushed the cart away and ran over to me, saying, "I am sorry, honey! Are you okay?"

I passed out.

After a while, I opened my eyes in a real daze, and found myself surrounded with many people, everyone saying, "Are you okay, honey? Are you good, sweetheart?"

I looked at the strange faces. I was amazed, and just kept looking at them. "*What's going on?*"

I said to myself. "*Did I do something wrong or what?*" I recognized my Aunt among the faces.

"What happened, Aunt?" I asked her.

"You fell down, honey, and hit your head on the floor," my Aunt said to me.

"Why are all these people around me?" I asked.

"They want to know if you are okay," said Aunt.

One of them said, "Let us take her to the hospital."

I said, "I am okay, Aunt, I do not want to go to the hospital. I'm scared of hospitals."

"No, honey, we will just do a checkup to know if you are okay," said Aunt.

"No, Aunty," I cried. "I am good, just a little pain in my leg but not too much."

Then my Aunt said, "Okay, honey; do not worry."

"Keep an eye on her for 24 hours; if there is something wrong, take her to the hospital," said an old man standing near us.

Then people helped me up, wished me well, and said goodbye to me, and we continued shopping. I was limping, but not too badly.

On the way home, I was not thinking about my pain, but I was thinking about the people who were surrounding me when I fell, and why they treated me like this, They were so friendly and kind to me!

"They are not Americans," I said to myself. I tried to convince myself of that until we arrived home.

When my mother saw my leg, she came to me anxiously, asking, "What happened, honey?"

My Aunt said, "She fell down in the market, but she is good, don't worry." At that time Yousuf came, and when he saw me, he said laughingly, "You don't even know how to walk."

"Yousuf, it is not funny," his mother said dryly. "If you don't have something good to say, be silent. Maryam, honey, go and rest on your bed, and I will bring ice to put on your leg."

Chapter 7

When I went to lay on my bed, I found a small envelope on the pillow. Quickly, I opened it and found a little red card in it.

Dear Maryam,

I received your letter, but I don't accept people from Africa.

Thanks,
Santa Claus

The letter fell from my hands, and I felt my heart fall with it. I cried so much. I heard my cousins laughing behind the door. I tore the card and threw it in the trash basket beside my bed. I threw with it my dreams and my friend's wishes, and I decided not to think about it anymore.

During dinner, my aunt's husband said, "Sorry, Maryam, for what happened today in the market."

"It is okay, Uncle," I said.

"Are you okay now?" he asked.

"Yes, uncle. I am so good," I answered.

"Everyone was scared about you in the shop," Aunty said.

I said with wonder, "They treated me nicely and with love. I am so happy about their concern."

Yousuf said, "They were concerned? Fake news, dad," and he laughed so much.

Everyone around the dinner table kept quiet. My aunt broke the silence and said, "Yes, they were so scared for her; all the people inside and outside the shop surrounded her and asked about her."

"This is not funny, Yousuf. I do not like your behavior," said his dad. "You need to say sorry to her now," he continued with anger.

Yousuf replied, "For what, Daddy? I…"

"I told you to say sorry now," his dad said, stopping Yousuf from speaking.

Then Yousuf squeaked, "Sorry, Maryam."

"Go and stay in your room, and your mom will bring your food there."

Yousuf screamed "Daddy!"

"Do what I said—go now!" said his dad loudly.

Yousuf stood up with tears in his eyes and was compelled to leave the table. After that, everyone finished the dinner and went to their beds to sleep.

Everyone slept except me; I was thinking about my day's events. I was so sad. I abandoned my dream to meet Santa Claus; now nothing was interesting on my holiday. I felt so bored because I had no good relationship with my cousins. I was not happy and not comfortable when I was playing with them, because they were bullying me. I hadn't faced rejection from anyone in my life; I love everyone, and all the people in my family, school, and neighborhood love me as well. So I was confused, and I asked myself, "*What is wrong? Am I wrong or is it them?*"

I carefully went to my mother where she was sleeping and woke her;. "Mom, mom!"

"Are you okay honey? What happened?" asked my mom with a sleepy voice.

"I am okay, mom, but I want to tell you something," I said. "I want to go back to our country; I don't want to stay here anymore."

Mom looked at me with wonder.

"People do not like us here in this country," I said.

"Why do you think like this?"

"Because of my cousins."

"Don't think like this, sweetie," she said. "We came to visit our family here; they all love us so much. Stop thinking about this and go back to your bed."

I went back to my bed, but I was still so sad when I laid on my bed, I couldn't hold back my tears. I kept crying for a long time until I fell asleep.

Chapter 8

In the morning, I opened my eyes in a bad mood, saying to myself, "Tomorrow is Christmas Eve; tomorrow night will be very disappointing,."

Hawa, who lay on the next bed asked me, "What did you say, now?"

I said, "Nothing." I would have a long day with the family; we were going to go shopping for the clothes that we would wear on Christmas Eve and Christmas Day.

In the clothes shop, I chose my clothes myself, but as usual, my cousins started laughing at me.

"Ew. African style," said Yousuf, and all three of them laughed loudly.

"I am proud to wear African style," I said and left the place. When I went to the fitting

room, there was a lady helping people inside; she smiled at me, saying, "You are so beautiful, and those clothes will be so pretty on you."

I smiled and asked her, "Do you like this style?"

"Yes, so much. I bought them for my daughter; the same shirt with the same pants," said the lady. "Even I was surprised when I saw them in your hands."

Then I felt that God sent this lady to me because I was really depressed, and my cousins

mistreated me. Then I squeaked, "Thank you, God." I tried them on; they were perfect on me.

I went back to the clothes section and chose another dress, because I had to get two outfits. After all the family bought clothes, we went back home. When we arrived, my mother and aunt started preparing the Christmas dinner.

On December 24th, I woke up early and felt so sad because this day was supposed to be my special day. I was calling it Santa's Night, but no more; a lot of things happened to make me forget my dream. I thought it would be easy, but from the minute I arrived, everything made me give up on my dream.

I prepared my clothes and got ready around 7 p.m. After I finished, I came out to the living room and sat with the family,

My Aunt's husband said to me, "Beautiful clothes. I like your style."

Yousuf squeaked, "Not fake news?"

His dad said, "What?"

Quickly, I said, "Thank you so much, Uncle."

All the family members were sitting around the table eating dinner happily, chatting, laughing, and wishing each other a happy Christmas. I was silent most of the time; I was thinking of my destroyed dream. After we finished dinner, my aunt's husband said: "This Christmas is the best Christmas ever since we came to America, because you are with us, and we hope all the family will be with us next year."

Aunt said, "We are so happy."

Aunt's husband continued, "We want everyone to say his or her wish. I will go first. I hope we are all together and in good health."

My Dad said, "Thank God, you gathered us, and I hope we will be together through all the coming years."

Then my Aunt said, "I hope we will be with our parents next year, and they are in good health,"

Everyone said, "Amen."

Then my Mom said, "I wish health, happiness, and joy for all the family,"

They said "Amen."

After that, the kids talked. Yousuf said, "I wish that Santa Claus would bring me a gun!"

When I heard this, I was surprised, but his father said, "You can't own a gun at this age, Yousuf."

"I will not use it, I will keep it until I am eighteen years old."

Then I asked, "Do you want to join the military or the police?".

Yousuf laughed so much, and then he said, "You are so naïve, Maryam."

My aunt's husband said to me, "People here own guns for personal protection."

I inquired, "Do you think owning a gun will keep you safe? I don't think so. Safety is to live with peace of mind, not to expect danger anytime."

Then Yousuf said, "You don't know about this, Maryam."

I said, "I know that people use guns when they are in the military or the police, and when there is war. Uncle Ahmed, the guard of our school, has a big cane, but never saw him holding a gun, and we feel so safe."

My aunt's husband said, "It is different from one country to another, Maryam."

I said, "But people at least are the same. If you kill someone, they had a soul, in Africa or in America—no difference." All of them became silent.

Then Ibrahim wanted Santa Claus to bring him an Xbox, and Hawa's wish was a cell phone. Then Aunt's husband said, "Maryam, why are you silent?"

I could not tell him I wished to meet Santa Claus, but I said, "I wish everyone in the world loved Africans because really, they are not bad, they are good people."

Yousuf squeaked, "Fake news." I heard him because I was sitting beside him.

After the family finished dinner, everyone went to bed because it was Santa's Night. I put on my pajamas and got into the bed. Really, I was so sad, because this night, I was supposed to wait for Santa Claus, but unfortunately, things hadn't gone as I wanted.

I was listening to my cousins talking about the gifts they would receive the next day; they were so happy and excited. I was thinking about what I would tell my friends; they would ask me about Santa. I cried until I fell asleep.

Chapter 9

I was sleeping deeply. Suddenly, I heard a whispered voice calling my name two or three times, I opened my eyes slightly. At first, I thought I was dreaming. I saw an old man with red clothes putting a hat on his head, and had a big white beard, he said to me: "Hi, Maryam."

I couldn't talk. I opened my eyes widely; he smiled and said to me: "Don't be scared honey; I am Santa Claus." I was so surprised I almost passed out. I didn't expect to see Santa Claus that night, but now Santa Claus and I both went outside to the living room.

I said absentmindedly, "How is it possible?"

"Are you not happy to see me?" he said.

"No, but I don't believe it after I gave up on my dream coming true!"

"This means you should never give up in your life, as long as you are alive."

I looked at him and said, "Yes, we have to have faith in God, because everything is in His hands."

"Don't think about a dream saying it is big, but think that God is the biggest and the greatest."

I smiled. "Yes, you are right. I always think like this."

He sat on the couch and asked me to sit beside him.

"Tell me your story, honey," he said.

I breathed deeply and started to tell him my dream. "I came with my parents to visit my aunt's family; we are from Africa. But my first reason to come here is to meet you. I heard a lot of stories about you from my cousins, but I am so mad at you!"

Putting his hand above my head, he said , "Why you are mad at me, honey?."

I said, sadly, "Because you ignored African children. Why don't you come to us? We also need to be happy during Christmas. We are good children just like the others; we have good behavior, although we do not live a luxurious life. We don't have school buses—we walk to school, and we don't have lunch boxes. Sometimes, we don't eat a meal at school, not even snacks, and some schools don't have desks, tables, or even chairs. We don't have clean, healthy, flushing toilets, and some children do not have good clothes. Despite all those things, we are happy and safe. We go to school, and we get an education, and we are all good children. We respect our families, we have clean hearts, and we accept all people. I never see myself as inferior to my cousins because I am from Africa."

Santa Claus felt so emotional! He said, trying to hold back his tears, "I am proud of you, Maryam. I didn't ignore African children, you ignored me," he said with a smile. "I tried to communicate with you, but I never received messages from African children," he continued, laughing, "I thought African children hated me."

I said, "how can that be possible, Santa?"

Then Santa Claus said to me, "I see sadness in your eyes; why?" I kept silent. He said "Do your cousins treat you well?" Then I covered my face with my hands and started to cry.

"Oh my God, my sweetheart, do not cry! I know everything."

"I am so happy I met them, but why are they so mean to me? I love them so much, but they do not love me."

"No, honey, they love you, but you didn't meet before, so you need time to get to know them. Give them time."

"But we are leaving next week."

"When you come next holiday, they will be good to you."

I asked Santa Claus, "Do you understand my talk clearly?"

"Yes, honey; why?"

"Because my cousins keep laughing at my pronunciation."

"You don't need to worry about them; you speak another language to communicate with people from a different background, and if they understand you, that's all that matters." Santa Claus looked at the clock on the wall in front of him. He stood up, drank the milk, took the candy and said: "I have to go, honey."

He left two boxes and wrote on them. I told him, "But my cousins are three, not two."

"These gifts are not for them; both of them are for you."

I tried to keep myself from screaming, but I couldn't. "For me?"

He said, "Yes, I received your message."

I said, "Thank you, God." I continued, "But Santa Claus, they will feel sad. I don't want them to feel sad, please."

He said, "After all they did, you care about them." I was silent, but he said, "Yes, honey, you have to be like this. We don't have a place for hatred in the world," He continued "Hatred is the fake news and love is the true news." He left a card near the Christmas tree with *Yousuf, Ibrahim, and Hawa* written on it. He gave me a hug and said, "See you in Africa, honey."

I said, "Let it be true news, not fake news, because my friends are waiting for you in Africa."

He said, "Yes, it will be true news, we will never let hatred and fake news ruin our lives."

"Pleas,e Santa Claus, wait; I want one more thing," I said.

"Tell me, honey," said Santa Claus.

"I want to touch your beard."

He laughed so much and let me touch his beard, and before leaving, he held my hand and said to me, "Dear, always remember this: We don't have to expect acceptance and good behavior from others. But for our soul to be restful and to live in peace, we have to understand and accept all people, even if they are different from us. Even if they mistreat us, we don't treat them the same way. We have to treat people according to our beliefs and our behavior, not by their behavior." Santa Claus released my hand and left.

I waved at Santa Claus until he disappeared, and I went back to my bed quietly. I wasn't even curious to see the gifts. I totally forgot about them; I was so happy that I met Santa Claus I wished to go back the next day to tell my friends about the miracle. The good news is that Santa Claus would come to Africa next year, but I would wait until next week to tell my friends the news—it was not so far away.

When I lay down on the bed, I was thinking how much I love God. He never let me down; whatever I wanted, He made it real. When I felt I couldn't meet Santa Claus, He made it possible. I have to be sure about God, not about the reality. I remembered the card, and I realized that my cousins wrote this card and gave it to me, but I didn't care.

Chapter 10

I woke up at the sound of my cousins' crying voices. For a while, I didn't know what was going on, but seconds later, I realized. I remembered what had happened last night; they were angry because of Santa Claus. I didn't get out of the bed; I waited until they were quiet, then took a quick shower, put on my new clothes, and went into the living room. When my Aunt saw me, she said happily, "Maryam, my sweetheart, Santa Claus left two gifts for you."

I acted as if I knew nothing, and said, "Really?"

"Yes, honey," said my Aunt.

But my mother said, "These gifts are for all of you."

My Aunt said, "No, they are for Maryam. Santa Claus knows who has good behavior and who has bad behavior."

I looked at the table and saw a card. I took it and read it.

Dear Yousuf, Ibrahim, and Hawa,

I am sorry because I did not leave gifts for you. I love you guys, and I want you to have better behavior. Try to treat others in the right way, because if we treat people well, this means we will be good, and if we mistreat people, this means we are bad. It depends on what type of person that you want to be. We have to treat all people equally and with respect, even if they are mean to us. It doesn't matter where you come from, or what color your skin is. What really matters is the values and the behavior that people conduct, because the names of places, colors of people, they are just terms given by people.

If people are different from us, this does not mean they are bad, or they are wrong. We have to accept all people and be good to them, not laugh at them and not bully them. Because in

everyone, there are good things and bad things; there is no one who is completely good, because we are human, so we have to look for the good things and try to ignore the bad things.

Yousuf, I am so sorry, I can't bring you a gun at any age, because when you are trying to protect yourself, you could put another person in danger.

Guys, it is so important to connect with our roots, because this is where we came from and it is a part of us. Roots need water, and if we

don't water them, they will die—and so will part of us. I hope to meet you next year in Africa.

Santa Claus.

I was not so happy because my cousins were sad. I hugged them and asked them to open the gifts together, so we opened them. The first box was an iPad and the second one was full of candy.

Then Yousuf said, "all of us have iPads; this is for you, Maryam."

I said with a smile, "And the candy is for you guys."

He said, "Sounds good," then we hugged each other.

After that, they said to me, "We are so sorry, Maryam. We were so mean to you. Please forgive us, because we wrote Santa's letter."

I said with tears, "It is okay. I love you guys so much."

Then Yousuf said, "African people are good people. It was fake news, and we will go there on our next holiday."

I said, "Really?"

Hawa said, "Yes, Daddy said so. We have to see our roots, and our grandparents."

At that time, my father and my Aunt's husband were outside, but they came inside the house. My aunt's husband was holding two envelopes in his hand. He said "There are two envelopes for you, Maryam—one of them from the lady who hit you yesterday. It's a $100 gift card. And the other one is from the market; it is a gift card worth $50."

I smiled and said, "American people are just like African people; both are pure, sensitive, and awesome. My dream came true! This is the real America. It is true news."

TO BE CONTINUED...
in

The Night Maryam Met Santa Claus

Part 2: Santa Claus in Africa